PAIGE DIXON

ı, who lives in the weste

nited States, has long had an ir.

in the out-of-doors and the animals tha

in the wild. Although he has often

forced to live in the city, it is the wilder pa

of the United States that have always been c

most interest. With his first book, *Lion on*

the Mountain, and this, he is now beginning

to translate that interest into books

dren and young people.

SILVER WOLF

UNIT E

SILVER WOLF

Paige Dixon

Illustrated by Ann Brewster

Atheneum / 1975 / New York

FOR

HELEN MAR

AND

FRIEND

Copyright © 1973 by Paige Dixon
All rights reserved
Library of Congress catalog card number 72-86932
ISBN *0-689-30083-2*
Published simultaneously in Canada by
McClelland & Stewart, Ltd.
Manufactured in the United States of America
by H. Wolff, New York
First Printing January 1973
Second Printing May 1975

SILVER WOLF

one

S ilver Wolf trotted down the incline of the fire lane and stopped at the bottom of the hill. In his six months of life this was the first time he had wandered away from the pack alone, but he was very hungry. He had caught one squirrel, pouncing on it with his front feet. One squirrel was not much of a meal. He was still hungry, but it had begun to snow, and he wanted to go home. He sniffed everywhere, trying to find the scent that would tell him he was in home territory.

He had never experienced snow, and it made him nervous. He quivered as the soft flakes fell cold and light on the silver guard hairs of his pelt, and melted into the black undercoat. He shook himself and moved in under some pines, but the snow sifted silently through the branches and down upon him.

Making a decision, he left his shelter and cut across a small clearing. He jumped the narrow stream that had already frozen along its edges. Nosing at an old, fire-blackened stump, he found what he was looking for, the smell of home. He broke into a quick trot, confident now that he was safe.

In a few minutes he reached the edge of the familiar open area that his pack had used for a rendezvous ever since they had moved away from the den. It was a long narrow stretch of meadow, its grasses and weeds flattened where he and his brother and sister played and wrestled. He saw his mother stretched out with her nose on her paws, her ears pricked forward alertly. His brother and sister trotted out to meet him, and his brother cuffed him, but he was not in the mood to play. He went over to his mother and peered down at her to see if she was frightened by the strange white stuff that floated down on them. She looked at him calmly with her slanted yellow eyes.

Silver Wolf's brother rolled on his back and tried to catch the snowflakes between his paws. Silver Wolf joined in the game, and in a few minutes all three pups were rolling and snapping and pretending to bite each other. They were already almost as big as adult wolves, but they were still clumsy.

On a rise above them, a two-year-old male, son

of the leader of the pack and second in authority, watched them play. Every few minutes he looked around expectantly. On the far edge of the clearing, an aging female wolf lay on her side, seeming to sleep.

Just visible over the western edge of the clearing, the sun came through the clouds, a white disk distinguishable from the whiteness of the sky only by its pale glitter. The snow dwindled to a few dancing flakes.

Then from nearby came a short, low-pitched howl. All the wolves, even the old female, got to their feet and bunched together, waiting. The leader of the pack trotted into the clearing, and at once they pressed forward to greet him, trying to nuzzle him, pushing each other aside in a frenzy of welcome, as if he had been gone a long time instead of just a few hours. The leader's son, slightly crouched, his tail held low and ears slanted back, licked the leader's muzzle and pawed the grass with his front left foot. The old female tried timidly to get into the welcome, but Silver Wolf's mother pushed her away. The younger wolves nipped at the leader's mouth, whimpering and crying on one note. Silver Wolf nipped a little too hard, and the leader jerked his head back, growling. The leader's son snapped at Silver Wolf.

The leader was a big tawny wolf, with a massive

head and watchful, intelligent eyes. He had taken over the pack when Silver Wolf's father was killed by a hunter. His son had come with him. Like the others, Silver Wolf followed the leader without question.

Now the leader was going to take them on a hunt. During the hot summer the pack hunted only at night when the air was cool, but now the weather was cold enough for daylight hunting.

It was the first time the pups had been allowed to go. Until now they had had to wait impatiently for their elders to return before they could eat. Sometimes Silver Wolf's mother brought back meat for the pups, or sometimes, as she had done when they were small, she regurgitated chunks of meat so the young ones could eat.

The leader started out of the clearing with a jaunty, self-confident gait, his step springy, his tail held high and waving. The others strung out behind him in single file, Silver Wolf between his brother and his sister. The old female kept her place far behind the others.

They followed their own trail around the shore of the lake that was just a few yards from their rendezvous. There was a freshening wind at their backs, and the small waves near the edge of the lake made a splashing sound as they washed up over the film of ice that rimmed the water. Silver Wolf made a quick detour to step onto the ice, which he was curious about. It broke under his feet, and he yipped with surprise when the cold water washed over his paws. He quickly rejoined the line of wolves.

The leader left the lake at its western end and started down a brushy game trail. Silver Wolf crowded his brother, just ahead of him, impatient to see what was going on in the front. His brother turned and nipped at his neck, and in an instant the two were tumbling together. Their mother turned back and cuffed them, and they obediently fell into place again. The old female, who had almost caught up with them when they stopped to scuffle, waited until there was again a distance between her and the rest of the pack. She was no longer a good hunter, and although the pack tolerated her, they didn't want her getting in the way.

Up ahead, the leader came to a stop. Silver Wolf and his brother and sister crowded up front to see what was happening. Below them was a canyon that opened out into a meadow on the other end. It was snowing again, and the late afternoon air had a thick milky look. Silver Wolf peered down into the canyon and saw what had stopped the leader. A moose stood at one side, his back to them, browsing on the twigs of the brush that grew out of the canyon wall. Perched grotesquely on his long skinny legs, the moose looked enormous.

The wolves huddled, touched each other's noses, wagged their tails. Coming down the trail they had barked every now and then, but now they were silent. After a moment they fell into single file again, and the leader began the descent into the canyon.

Silver Wolf was quivering with excitement and the possibility of food. When a big hare leaped aside from the trail and hopped into the woods on his floppy feet, Silver Wolf didn't even turn.

As the wolves, still strung out in single file, silently stalked the moose, the huge animal, unaware of them, raised up on his thin hind legs to reach a dwarf willow. With his body he pulled the willow down and held it under his forefeet while he ate. He was so intent on his food that he didn't notice the wolves until they were within fifty feet of him.

With a movement surprisingly swift for such an awkward-looking animal, the bull moose whirled around to face them. The wolves stopped in their tracks, and for a full minute the moose and the leader stared at each other, tense and unmoving. Then abruptly the leader sat down. The leader's son, behind him, also sat down. Silver Wolf growled softly in his throat, his muscles quivering. He waited for the attack that he knew must come.

The moose was very big, with antlers six feet across. He must have weighed over twelve hundred pounds. Although he was alert, he didn't seem frightened. He had a long dark face with a floppy muzzle and a bell of skin that flapped under his chin. His large ears hung limp. He had white nostrils and white circles around his eyes, and the lower parts of his legs were white, but otherwise he was a dull brown. The stiff mane, that stood up when he was alarmed, bristled now.

For some time neither side moved. Then with a sudden coughing grunt the moose wheeled and raced down the canyon in a fast, long-stepping trot. Instantly the wolves were after him. For the length of the canyon they were close to him, gaining on him, but as soon as the moose broke out into the meadow, he went into a long gallop, feet bunched together.

The wolves increased speed too, their heads lowered and pointing toward the moose. For a quarter of a mile they chased him, trying to get close enough to attack, but then, so suddenly that the pups fell over the older wolves, the chase ended.

Silver Wolf's hopes for a full stomach faded as quickly as they had begun. He would have liked to go on after the moose, risking the savage blows of the sharp hoofs, but he knew that he must do as the leader did. So he sat down and waited.

After a while, lifting his nose to the wind, the leader started off again, diagonally across the meadow toward the woods on the other side. Silver

Wolf could see nothing, but soon he too caught the scent of moose, and he pushed to get closer to the front of the line. But his mother snapped at him to keep him in place.

A cow moose and her calf were lying in the tall grass at the edge of the meadow. As the wolves approached, she lumbered to her feet. Her stubby, three-inch tail switched and she lowered her long head, as she moved between the wolves and her calf. It was a big calf, already about three hundred pounds, and it kept moving away from its mother's protective flanks to see what was happening.

As the wolves pressed closer, the cow charged the leader. He sprang away and moved quickly back and forth in an evasive action. The calf bellowed as Silver Wolf's mother darted in and nipped its flank. The cow swerved and started for the protection of the trees, trying to move the calf in ahead of her, but the calf was panicky now and he didn't do what she wanted. As Silver Wolf's mother headed for him again, the calf gave a wild bleat and floundered into the woods. The cow tried to follow, but the leader cut her off and drove her back into the clearing, springing at her flanks in big bounds. Only the leader and his son attacked; the others watched, Silver Wolf trembling with excitement.

The cow moose struck out with wicked hoofs as the wolves attacked. Silver Wolf's mother joined the attack; and in spite of her skill, she was struck in the shoulder by a flying hoof. She fell into the snow and lay still for a few minutes, while the two males continued the attack. Silver Wolf went to his mother and nuzzled her, and in a moment she staggered to her feet.

The leader's son sprang at the moose's face and caught her big rubbery nose between his teeth. The cow swung her head, trying to shake him loose, but he held on, swinging in the snowy air. Then, staggering under the leader's attack, the moose fell and almost instantly died.

The hungry wolves ate for the first time in many days. Silver Wolf had already learned that a wolf's life was one of feast or famine: he could live many days without food, but when food was available, as it was now, he would eat all that his stomach would hold, sometimes as much as twenty pounds in two or three days.

The old female sat at one side, watching while the wolves ate. Finally she moved in cautiously, seeking her share, but the leader's son snapped at her and she withdrew. In a little while hunger drove her back again. She pulled a chunk of meat away from the others and ate, watching warily to make sure they didn't drive her off.

When the wolves had eaten their fill for the time being, they drank thirstily from the cold water of a

nearby stream, and then, on the edge of the meadow where they could guard the rest of the meat, they flopped down on the snowy ground to sleep.

The next day they alternately ate and slept. That night a wolf from another pack tried to get some of their meat, but the wolves drove him off, and the leader's son chased him until he disappeared in the forest.

On the third day the sun came out brightly, and the clouds trailed off. The air was cold, and when Silver Wolf stepped on the snow it made a crunching sound that startled him.

When nothing was left of the kill except the skin and bones, the pack started diagonally across the sunlit meadow. They were near the middle of the open space when they heard a strange noise, a roar that came from the sky. The leader stopped and tried to catch the scent of whatever it was, but there was no scent that he recognized. He continued on across the meadow, watching warily. Behind them the ravens had gathered around the bones of the moose, and overhead a hawk circled the tops of the pines, but there was nothing else to be seen.

Then the roar grew very loud, and a plane swooped toward them. To the wolves it looked like a huge bird. They broke into a fast run, but the thing in the sky was much faster. It dipped low over them, glittering silver in the sun and filling the meadow with its noise and smell. The leader hesitated, confused. Then he lowered his head and ran for the shelter of the forest, the others still in single file behind him.

The plane circled the meadow and flew over them again. This time there was a new sound, like quick bursts of thunder. Just ahead of Silver Wolf, his sister leaped suddenly sideways and fell in the snow, blood gushing from her neck. Again the plane circled and came back.

The wolves broke rank and raced for the trees. This time the gunfire left small black holes in the snow, but no other wolf fell.

When they reached the sanctuary of the woods, Silver Wolf looked back. The murderous thing from the sky was coming to earth, gliding in and landing, bumping along until it came to a stop. Silver Wolf's sister lay still, a dark figure on the white snow.

two

In the shelter of the forest, the wolves fanned out and headed for their camp in twos and threes. Behind them the roar of the plane had been cut off, but the strong, unpleasant smells that hung in the air irritated Silver Wolf's sensitive nose. Following his mother, he circled around and came back to a wooded hill where they could look down, unseen, on the meadow below. His mother lay low to the ground, her nose pointed toward the clearing.

Two men had climbed down from the plane and were huddled over the dead wolf. The blade of a knife flashed as one of them held it up and brought it down again. Silver Wolf didn't know what they were doing, but he shivered and crept closer to his mother.

16

One of the tall dark figures stood up, holding the head and skin of the dead wolf. They clambered back into the silver bird, and the sound of the roar and the sickening smell of smoke streamed from it. Silver Wolf crept further back into the trees. The plane moved down the field, lifted off, and climbed into the sunny sky.

For some time Silver Wolf's mother didn't move. Silver Wolf came close to her, nuzzling her. She got to her feet at last and stood sniffing the air from all directions. Then slowly she went down into the meadow, to the blood-soaked place in the snow where her pup had lain. She moved around and around the spot, making whimpering sounds in her throat. Ravens hovered in the air above the bones, and Silver Wolf snarled at them.

After a while the long howl of the leader came through the forest, calling the pack together. Answering howls came from other parts of the woods, and Silver Wolf's mother too lifted her head and howled, a long note that blended with the voices of the others to make a strange music. Silver Wolf added his voice to the singing. It was time for the wolves to come together. His mother touched a patch of red snow with her nose, then turned and headed for home. Silver Wolf followed her.

Three of the ravens flapped after them, diving down at Silver Wolf, teasing him. He nipped at them. He was used to ravens; they always hovered near the wolves, waiting for a meal of leftovers. In a few minutes they wheeled and flew back to the meadow.

The howling of the pack grew louder as those who had wandered away returned to the rendezvous. Silver Wolf stopped every few minutes to turn his nose skyward and howl.

As soon as all the wolves had gathered, the leader started north, into the deeper woods. They were not going to their old rendezvous. With man so close it was no longer safe.

Once more they moved further north, deeper into the forest. They traveled through the woods, around lakes, once even swimming the cold waters of a river when it proved to be the only way to reach the other shore. On the way, the leader and his son killed an old, crippled doe, and the pack feasted. At no time did the leader take his pack across an open field.

At last they came to a small, deep-green lake surrounded by dense stands of ponderosa pine. Near the northern end of the lake, in a place where a forest fire had partly cleared a space at some time, the pack found a new home. Silver Wolf and his mother and brother made a shelter beside a deadfall, under the crossed trunks of two blackened, half-fallen trees. The snow here was deeper than it had been in their old home, and the air was colder.

There were deer not far from the lake, and within half a day's journey an elk herd that the deepening snow had driven to lower ground in search of food. Whenever possible, the leader took the pack after old and ailing deer, who were easy to catch. Silver Wolf became skilled in attack as he grew bigger and older and less clumsy.

As the winter lengthened, his coat grew thicker, and he grew until he was almost as big as the leader's son. By midwinter the leader's son sometimes had to remind Silver Wolf who was boss. Except for his father, the leader of the pack, the leader's son was the dominant male in the pack. Silver Wolf's brother never forgot it, and when the leader's son came toward him, he would roll over on his back or curl his tail alongside his legs and lower his head to show that he knew his place. But Silver Wolf found it harder and harder to act that way.

One bright afternoon when Silver Wolf had been down near the lake catching a snowshoe rabbit, he met the leader's son on the trail that the wolves had already worn between the lake and their new home. The leader's son stopped and stared at Silver Wolf, the hard challenging stare of the dominant animal. He was not seriously threatening. Within the pack there were no real hostilities; it was the look by which the older wolf reminded Silver Wolf who he was. With his tail up and his yellow eyes unblink-

ing, he waited for Silver Wolf to duck his head and move aside, or even to turn his back toward him in submission.

But this time Silver Wolf stared back. For a long moment the two wolves glared at each other. Then the leader's son began a warning growl. His ears came up, his tail trembled, and his mane bristled. He took a step toward Silver Wolf and bared his teeth. Then he crouched, as if he meant to spring. Silver Wolf stood his ground, hunching his back into a curve, holding his head back and his ears flat to his head. He too bared his teeth and snapped, and then snapped again, his teeth close to the muzzle of the other wolf. Then as abruptly as it had started, the challenge ended. Almost together the two wolves turned away from each other and went on about their business. Nothing had been settled.

There was much snow that winter and finding food was hard. Sometimes they had to flounder through chest-deep snow in their search. But the snow also made escape difficult for their prey, and if the wolves could reach the area where the deer were, they were sometimes successful. When the wolves traveled in the snow, Silver Wolf learned to keep in the tracks of the wolf ahead of him; each one did this, so that the marks they left in the snow looked as if they had been made by one animal with big feet.

One night there was a break in the weather. A warm chinook wind blowing in from the faraway west coast melted snow and sent temperatures up fifty or sixty degrees overnight. Because he was hungry, Silver Wolf decided in the morning to go out alone, although until that time he had not wandered far from the others in the silent, snowbound forest.

The ground was wet and slushy under his feet, and above him the big pines dripped melting snow. The unexpected warmth made him feel good. He trotted along the edge of the stream, where already there were some thin places in the ice, awash with water. He found a hole in the river bank that had once been some animal's den; but although he sniffed at it, he could find nothing to eat and no recent scent. Once he stopped and pricked his ears forward, listening intently, as the lightest echo of an unfamiliar sound drifted to him on the warm wind. He stood still listening for several minutes, but he didn't hear it again.

At a bend in the creek he passed under a choke-cherry tree and jumped nervously as the branches unloosed a shower of water on his back. The bark on the tree had been chewed by a bear or a deer, and many of the berries were gone. But to a wolf, bark and berries were not real food. He needed meat.

He was further from home now than he had ever been alone. When he came to a beaver house in the frozen water, he pawed at it, but the frozen twigs and chunks of bark refused to budge. A little way from it, the ice was thin and he could see black water under it. He sniffed at it, but the ice broke under his touch and frightened him. He snuffed the water away from his nose and went back to the safety of the bank. He lay down and watched the hole and rested.

He was half-drowsing when a sudden movement on the ice caught his attention. He stiffened and watched. A black nose appeared in the open place in the creek, and then a sleek wet head came up out of the water. A beaver climbed up onto the ice, breaking through and swimming to a firmer place. Silver Wolf lay very still, watching the beaver as it waddled to the opposite side of the stream and climbed up onto the wet, slushy bank.

As the beaver started into the woods, Silver Wolf crept out onto the ice, keeping his eyes on the fat beaver. The animal, unaware of danger, stopped to nibble on some twigs, then hitched along further into the woods. Silver Wolf felt the cold water of the melting ice beneath his toes, but his mind and his eyes were on the beaver. He moved close to the dam that the beaver had built across the stream and slunk along almost on his stomach.

Without warning there was a loud crack, and the ice beneath him gave way. Doused in the cold water, he floundered to get out. The beaver raced for the safety of his house, and with a slap of his broad tail he disappeared into the watery entrance before Silver Wolf could reach him. Silver Wolf shook the cold water from his coat and pawed at the beaver's house, whining softly in his disappointment.

Convinced at last that the beaver was out of reach, he turned to go home. But again he heard the strange plinking sound that he had heard before. It seemed to come from further up the stream. Curious, he moved silently through the brush that bordered the stream, the beaver already forgotten.

The warm steady wind was at his back, and no scent came to him from the direction of the strange sound. A squirrel, in a frenzy of delight at the false spring, danced out of his way and raced up a tree. Further away, a crow cawed hoarsely. And still the plinking sound continued, louder now.

Silver Wolf came around a bend in the stream and stopped short, shrinking back into the shelter of heavy brush. Set back from the water's edge in a little clearing was a small log cabin, its sides dark with the water that was dripping from the snow-covered roof. A man knelt near the door, chipping ice from a mound of dirt.

As the wind shifted, Silver Wolf got the full scent of man and recognized it as the smell of danger once more caught up with him. He hugged the ground and began very slowly backing away.

three

Silver Wolf stopped. Another smell came to him, competing with the offensive smell of man. It was the scent of fox. Torn between hunger and fear, he hesitated. Then slowly he crept back toward the cabin and settled down in a patch of tall ferns, where he could see the man without getting too close.

The man put down the pick he had been using to chop ice, and with his gloved hands he pushed aside the slush and dirt. Out of a depression in the ground he carefully lifted a piece of hide about three feet square. Holding it by its corners he disappeared inside the cabin. In a few minutes he came out again with the hide, a steel trap, and a small cloth bag. Then he walked into the woods. The fox smell and the man smell grew fainter.

Because he was both hungry and curious, Silver Wolf followed the man, moving like a shadow through the woods, keeping a safe distance.

After some time the man stopped, and Silver Wolf stopped too. The man was digging in the wet dirt near a faintly marked game trail. Silver Wolf inched forward to see what he was doing. He watched the rhythmic up-and-down motions the man made with the pick. The man was kneeling on the piece of hide that he had unearthed back at the cabin, and the dirt he took from the hole he was digging was dumped onto the hide. When he had finished digging, he picked up the big trap, set it in the hole he had made, and fastened it to the ground with a stake-pin. When everything was in place, he carefully built up a shoulder of dirt around the trap and covered it.

He took what dirt was left and carried it some distance from the trap, scattering it, so that the area around the trap showed no signs of having been dug into. When he came back, he bent over a low bush a few inches from the trap and emptied the contents of the cloth bag. He straightened up and took off his gloves.

"O.k., Mr. Fox," he said aloud. "Come on in." He picked up the hide and swished it around where he had been standing, and then he started back toward his cabin.

Silver Wolf could hear him whistling as he went

through the forest. The wolf waited a long time, until the only sounds anywhere around were the birds' occasional chirpings. Then, moving with great care, he went toward the place where the man had been.

There was a strong smell of fox at the bush where the man had dumped the little bag, but there was no fox, no meat for a hungry wolf. Although he had never seen a trap before, he instinctively stayed away from the place where it was buried.

He went back to his hiding place to wait. He waited until it was almost dark, not sure what it was he was waiting for. But nothing happened, and finally he went home, making a wide sweep around the man's cabin.

That night the temperature dropped again, and all the trees and bushes, the ferns and weeds, were coated with silver. The pack hunted for almost a week before they found food. Silver Wolf hunted with the pack, and sometimes he went alone as well. An occasional rabbit was all he could find. He grew gaunt, and he could think of nothing but food. Sometimes he went back to the beaver den, but the water had frozen over and there was no sign of the beaver, huddled below the ice in his winter home. In several places he found the round holes in the snow that voles make as they burrow down to the earth, but he found no voles that he could get at.

Once he came upon a muskrat's lodge near the

edge of a pond, and he poked at it. It was a big, cone-shaped affair, almost five feet across at the bottom, tapering up to three feet at the top, made of mud and sticks, with cattails growing tall all around it. Silver Wolf pawed and bit at the structure, but, like the beaver's lodge, he could make no dent in it.

Further on, he saw a porcupine who had just made a meal of the inside bark of a pine tree. Silver Wolf came as close as he dared. The porcupine arched his back and tucked his head between his front legs, keeping his back toward Silver Wolf in order to strike out with his spiny tail if the wolf came too near. Silver Wolf tried to circle him, but the porcupine moved too, keeping that dangerous tail ready to strike. Silver Wolf gave up and went on his way. For a while a big gray jay followed him, curious to see what he was up to, swooping down boldly, almost touching Silver Wolf, then up again to float lightly just above the trees, now and then giving his loud whistle.

A pileated woodpecker, big as a crow, was stripping bark off part of a dead tree and starting to hack out the big rectangular hole that he needed to find the wood-boring beetles he liked to eat. As Silver Wolf came along, the bird climbed higher up the tree, the red crest showing bright against his black plumage, his white wing patches visible only when he spread his wings and hovered near the tree, calling a loud "yuk yuk yuk" of annoyance at being interrupted.

Silver Wolf trotted along, the ice-laden bushes making small snapping sounds as he brushed against them. After a while he stopped and ate some red berries, though they did almost nothing to satisfy his hunger.

He slowed down as he came closer to the man's cabin, smelling again the man-smell and the fox-smell. As he had done before, he crept up carefully until he could see the cabin without being seen. There was no sign of the man, but smoke was coming out of the chimney of the cabin. At one side there was a big improvised wooden rack with three fox skins hanging on it.

Even though the man was nowhere in sight, Silver Wolf kept hidden, moving around the cabin on the three wooded sides. He could smell deer meat, but at first he saw no evidence of deer. Then in the back of the cabin, off a little way in the woods, he discovered the source of the smell. A haunch of venison hung from a tree. In spite of his intense hunger, Silver Wolf waited a long time to make sure the man was not around. Then, moving along warily almost on his stomach, he approached the venison.

On his first jump he didn't reach it. He tried again and caught the end of it in his teeth, but it

was partly frozen and slippery, and he lost his hold. He crouched and sprang once more. This time his strong canine teeth caught hold and he hung on, swinging. His weight pulled the meat loose, and he and the venison fell to the ground together. He pulled the meat off into the woods and tore into it hungrily. Because of the recent thaw it was hard-frozen only in the center. Remembering to keep a careful watch for the man, Silver Wolf ate and ate until he could eat no more. When he finished, most of the meat was gone.

He drank thirstily from the narrow, fast-moving stream that was only thinly skimmed with ice. He wanted to lie down and sleep, but it would be dangerous to sleep here. He went deeper into the woods, away from the faint trail he had made when he came. When he could no longer smell man, he lay down and slept.

four

The deep cold of late winter wrapped the forest in a long silence. The snow was frozen so hard that when Silver Wolf walked on it, his steps left hardly a trace. In the woods the sap froze in the trees, making them explode in sudden loud bursts like gunfire. Even the big river, up near where the elk were, finally froze solid.

The elk were forced even further down into the lowlands in search of food, and the wolf pack traveled the long distance to the aspen grove where a huge bull elk and his herd of sixteen cows searched for berries and chewed on the aspen and willow. Two smaller bulls lurked in the cover of pines and brush, keeping out of the way of the king bull. But there was almost nothing left there for them to eat; even the fungus was gone. The big, blockily built bull kept careful watch over the cows to make sure none of them wandered off with one of the younger bulls.

As the wolves waited behind their leader, a sound that they remembered came to them. It was the drone of a plane. Instantly the wolves melted into the protection of the forest, like shadows. The leader left the place and started the long journey back home, but for a few minutes Silver Wolf lingered, both frightened and curious.

A big plane flew in low over the field where the elk had been. All but one cow had already galloped heavily into the shelter of the woods, and as the plane came still lower, she followed them. When the plane was over the middle of the clearing, a bale of hay fell from it, landing with a thud on the snow. The plane circled the field and dropped another bale. Then it climbed, circled, and disappeared.

When the throb of its engine could no longer be heard, the bull elk came out from his hiding place and went up to the hay. The cows followed him, and even the two young bulls found a place at the second bale, away from the big bull. Hungrily they tore at the stiff hay.

If the wolf pack had been there, it would have been possible perhaps to ambush one of the older cows while the moose were all busy eating, but Silver Wolf could do nothing alone, and he was worried about the plane. He watched for a while and then followed the trail along the broad river that took him home.

A willow ptarmigan in his white winter coat followed him part of the way, swooping down low toward his head and scolding in his crowlike cackle. Silver Wolf snapped at him, and finally he flew away.

It took Silver Wolf a long time to go home, because he kept finding things he wanted to explore. Once he found a fox's den that his nose told him had been used recently, but although he waited a long time, no fox returned.

He went around by the man's cabin to see if there were any more venison haunches hanging from the trees. There were none, but several pelts had been added to the fox hides that he had seen there before: two mink skins and the skin of a fisher. Around at the side of the cabin there was now a wire cage, with a young gray lynx with light spots on his coat. When he saw Silver Wolf, he swished his bobbed tail threateningly and made a low growling sound in his throat.

Silver Wolf went on out to the place where he had seen the man set the trap. As he came near, he heard a sound and smelled a strong animal smell. Moving silently in the protection of the trees, he saw a wolverine finishing off the remains of a fox caught in the trap. The yellow-brown wolverine, almost as big as a small bear, had broad, light-colored stripes down his sides, and a bushy tail that twitched rhythmically as he enjoyed his meal.

Suddenly the wolverine whirled around, his small ears flat, his teeth bared. He had caught the scent of the wolf. Making not a sound, Silver Wolf slipped deeper into the woods and headed for home. He knew better than to bother a wolverine.

As he got near home, he heard the long howl of the leader, calling them together. Almost at once came the howl on a lower note that was the voice of Silver Wolf's mother. Then the high clear note of the leader's son, and the note just below it that belonged to Silver Wolf's brother. Silver Wolf himself stopped, gave one long sustained howl, and then hastened his pace toward home.

His brother arrived just ahead of him, and when Silver Wolf got there, the wolves were howling in chorus, brushing up against each other, wagging their tails. Silver Wolf ran to join them, making eager little sounds, ready to join the group.

The leader began to prance around Silver Wolf's mother, wagging his tail and going down on his front knees like a pup. He nipped her ears and her face and rubbed his head against hers. Whimpering in a low gentle voice, Silver Wolf's mother danced away from the leader and then came in close to him again, putting her neck across his shoulders. They

had been behaving this way for about a week now, and Silver Wolf had stopped being curious. The leader's son sometimes tried to court Silver Wolf's mother too, but his father pushed him aside, and he soon gave up.

Silver Wolf's brother caught Silver Wolf's paw in his teeth, in the way the wolves used for greeting. Silver Wolf pushed his head against his brother's shoulder and then the two of them raced around the clearing, roughhousing and chasing each other the way they had done when they were younger. Once Silver Wolf leaped over the old female, who was sleeping at the far end of the clearing. She started up nervously and then settled down again to continue her nap.

The two brothers played for a long time and finally fell asleep, tired out.

five

Silver Wolf and his brother went hunting together on a cold, quiet, sunny day. All morning they hunted and found nothing but berries and one rabbit. Toward noon they picked up the scent of deer, and quickening their pace, they started after it. If it was just one deer, and if it happened to be too old or too young to outrun them, they might be in luck. But if it should be a healthy buck or a fast-running doe, they would come away still hungry.

They ran silently, on their toes, Silver Wolf ahead of his brother. Suddenly they both stopped. Somewhere behind them there was a whining roar, like the sound of a plane, only it was not in the sky. Frightened, Silver Wolf's brother floundered into brush and sank to his chest in deep snow. In a min-

38

ute he got himself out, and stood trembling, waiting for Silver Wolf.

Silver Wolf stood very still, trying to tell just where the noisy thing was. It was coming toward them fast. He pushed his brother with his nose, and the two of them jumped a small frozen stream and moved part way up a hill, where they huddled out of sight in a stand of young pines. They lay down and waited

In a few minutes two snowmobiles came roaring along the game trail that the wolves had just left. The men stopped and got off, leaving their motors running. One of them bent over and studied the ground while the other one slapped his arms against his sides. Their breath made frosty traces in the cold air.

"See anything?" They had to yell to make themselves heard.

"Something, all right." The man who had been looking at the ground stepped to the side of the trail. "Snow's so hard, you can't hardly see the tracks, but something was along here just lately."

"Deer?"

The man stepped across his machine and examined the ground on the other side. "Hey, yeah! Here's a place where their hoofs broke the crust!"

"What's all that?" The other man pointed his mittened hand toward the broken snow where Silver

Wolf's brother had floundered.

The first man examined it, sinking down himself to his knees. "Hard to say." He bent down. "Could have been a wolf."

"Wolf! Who needs a wolf."

The first man, climbing out of the loose snow, laughed. "Scare you, Jack?"

The man called Jack swung back onto his machine. "I ain't scared. But I came out here to get me a deer. Can't do much with a wolf for dinner."

The first man came back and got on his machine. "Don't worry, a wolf's scareder of you than you are of him. If there's one around, you won't even see him. There's bound to be deer around here. Let's go."

The engines screamed louder and higher, and the men took off down the trail.

Silver Wolf and his brother lay still where they were, their noses wrinkling at the evil smell of the snowmobiles. They stayed there a long time, afraid to move, listening to the noise that grew fainter and finally died out. There was a path of snow that the machines had torn up and packed down hard. Smoke still hung in the air.

After some time there was a new sound, the sound of a large animal running recklessly through brush. The two wolves tensed and waited. Now they could hear the snowmobiles again, from some distance beyond the sound of the animal.

In a few minutes a doe came crashing through the forest, running blindly, smashing into trees. She passed on the narrow game trail below Silver Wolf and his brother. Her sides were heaving, and she was covered with sweat. She struck a tree and stood still for a moment, quivering all over, shaking her head from side to side. The high-pitched noise of the snowmobiles grew steadily louder. Staggering, the doe ran on.

In a few seconds the snowmobiles passed where Silver Wolf was concealed. They churned up the snow and filled the air with their racket and their foul smells. Then the noise stopped abruptly. Silver Wolf could hear the men yelling to each other.

"Hold it!" one of them shouted. "No need for a bullet. She's run herself to death."

The other man gave a yell of triumph, and then there was a long silence, broken now and then by the voices of the men. The combined smell of man and machine and deer was heavy in Silver Wolf's nose, like the smell of death. He and his brother lay perfectly still.

After some time the machines started up again, then faded from hearing. Still the wolves stayed where they were. At last, cautiously, they moved along the side of the game trail, taking care to stay hidden. They came to a place where the smoke from

the machines had turned the snow black. Just past the blackness a big patch of red stained the snow, and Silver Wolf found a few hairs from the coat of the doe. Nothing else remained.

six

The snowmobiles had frightened the deer from their winter feeding area; they had scattered far to the north. The wolves too were ready to move; to find or make a den where Silver Wolf's mother could have her new pups.

The leader took them a long way, to the banks of the big river, where they dug two dens, not far apart, in the sandy soil that the early spring thaws had begun to soften up. The oval-shaped entrance to one den was almost two feet across, and beyond it a slightly larger tunnel led to a little room about a dozen feet in the earth. Silver Wolf liked to explore the dens and to roll in the mound of dirt outside the entrance.

The rest of the pack found beds for themselves

44

on the hillside, above the den that Silver Wolf's mother was using. From there they could see any danger that might approach.

The old female moved in closer to the pack now, and the wolves no longer drove her off. Sometimes she lay at the mouth of the large den, moving stiffly aside when Silver Wolf's mother came in or went out.

The weather was warmer, and after a night-long chinook, the ice in the river began to break up. For days it boomed and crunched, as huge chunks broke loose and buckled, grinding against other ice or against the snow-mixed dirt along the shoreline. Black water spread thinly at first and then came with a rush from the broken places.

Coming across the river on solid ice, Silver Wolf was almost thrown into icy water when the place where he stood broke free and became a bucking, plunging, slippery danger under his feet. He barked sharply with fear and fought to keep his balance as the ice tilted and smashed into another chunk. A widening space of black water separated him from the safety of the river bank. Water drenched him. For a few moments the ice he stood on, barely big enough to hold him, sped down a channel of open water. Then with a smash that threw him off his feet, it hit a larger floe.

Silver Wolf struggled to his feet and jumped onto

the larger piece of ice. From there he was able to jump again to the stationary ice that lined the shore. In a few minutes he leaped onto the river bank. He shook himself hard, sending off a spray of cold water, and then he climbed the hill and lay down in the sunshine near his bed. Over his head, through the tops of the tall balsam, he saw a V-shaped formation of Canada geese coming back to the north country. Spring had come.

Downriver, the beavers began to venture forth from their winter dens, but they were too smart for Silver Wolf. They stayed close to the water, and at the first sign of danger, they dove into the river with a flat smack of their broad tails and disappeared from his sight.

It was still cold, especially at night, but the forest stirred with life. Ground squirrels came out of their burrows, scolding the whole forest with their sik-sik-sik. Woodchucks hunted near the river for grass, swimming to the other side when Silver Wolf saw them and tried to catch one. And the woodchuck's relative, the yellow-bellied marmot, bigger than his cousin and with a yellow-brown face, sought the same feeding ground. The lemmings came out to look for berries and roots, and the snowy owls looked for lemmings. The long, slender, brown marten, who had been abroad all winter, competed with the hungry wolves for squirrels, mice, and birds.

Silver Wolf came across the fur-lined nest of a white ermine, but the ermine was at home, and he hissed and squealed and chattered at Silver Wolf with such ferocity that the wolf went away.

Silver Wolf and his brother came upon some moulting ducks in a patch of tall grass, and made a meal of them. And one day Silver Wolf caught a grayling that had floundered out of the water onto the ice. But usually they went after big game, not bothering the smaller animals unless they were unable to find a deer or an elk or a moose. The elk had moved up to higher ground now that the heavy snow was melting, but there were still deer and an occasional moose.

Once, when hunting had been poor, Silver Wolf and his brother went to the cabin of the trapper. Again there was venison hanging from a tree but it was higher up this time, and neither Silver Wolf nor his brother could reach it. They jumped and jumped, frustrated and angry at being unable to reach the meat that was so close.

The big cage that had held the young lynx was empty, but there was a silvery lynx pelt spread out on the drying rack. The fox hides were gone, but there were beaver skins and a muskrat.

Silver Wolf approached the cabin very cautiously because the wind was at their backs and he couldn't count on smelling the man. But there was no sight or sound of anyone, so, bolder, he reached up and pulled at the lynx pelt with his teeth.

He heard the door open, and in an instant he was running for the woods, where his brother had already disappeared. The hot raking pain in his shoulder and the simultaneous roar of the man's gun caught him before he reached safety. He leaped sideways, under the impact of the bullet, and then flung him-

self into the brush as the gun exploded again. The second bullet screamed past him and sank into the trunk of a yellow pine.

Silver Wolf ran through the woods for a long time. At last, when he felt safe, he stopped and chewed at the place on his shoulder that hurt him. Blood soaked his fur, and he tasted its salty tang. His whole leg ached from the wound, but he was still able to run.

He continued on to the big river, and followed one of the trails the pack had made, until he came to the den. His mother came out and sniffed at his wound. His brother had already returned and was lying in the sun, still panting from his long run. Silver Wolf lay down beside him.

For several days the wound pained him and his leg was stiff, but then the discomfort went away and he almost forgot about it, except that he stayed away from the trapper's cabin.

seven

The snow was all gone except for hard patches under the trees, where the sun couldn't get at it, and the days were mild. Silver Wolf's mother had been staying in her den for several days, sleeping most of the time. One evening when the three-quarter moon seemed to be hung on the point of the tallest pine, she had her puppies. It took almost three hours, and when it was over, Silver Wolf had three new sisters and two brothers.

His mother lay down, tired, and curled her body protectively around the tiny, dark-furred pups. None of them weighed more than a pound. They had small round heads with tiny ears and blunt noses, eyes shut tight. At this age they could neither see nor hear.

Silver Wolf now spent most of his days near the den, watching the little pups. At night he went hunting with the pack, and if they were successful, he helped to bring back food for his mother.

After about a week the pups, still blind, began to crawl around on their front legs, whimpering and yipping. They drank a good deal of milk from their mother, and already they were beginning to grow.

When another week had gone by, they had their eyes open, but they still could not see well, and they stumbled about the den, falling over things and bumping into each other. The leader came to the den often, as Silver Wolf did, to play with the pups, and to help feed and clean them when they were old enough to eat meat. The old female was often there, and no one drove her off, for now she was useful, helping with the pups.

Silver Wolf's mother began to join the pack occasionally when it went on a hunt. One night when the wolves were following the river, the leader stopped. As it always did, the whole line stopped and waited. Slowly and carefully, the leader angled off the trail a short distance and sat down again. Silver Wolf moved in close behind him and caught the smell of deer meat. Walking almost on tiptoe, the leader approached a big chunk of venison that lay on the ground. He stopped again, then circled it, while the others watched him. Then he backed away sud-

denly, the hair along his neck bristling. He backed
up until he was on the trail again, and went on past
the place where the meat was.

The others followed him, but Silver Wolf was
curious. He swung off the path and went close to the
meat, sniffing the ground. He stiffened and stopped.
Very faint but unmistakable, the man-smell was
there. As the leader had done, he carefully backed
away from the invisible trap and caught up with
the pack.

When the pack came back that way later, having
found no deer, Silver Wolf's brother strayed from
the line toward the piece of deer meat that lay so
temptingly on the ground. His mother barked sharply
and trotted after him, pushing him back into line
with her head.

A little further along the trail the leader stopped
again and held his head high, sniffing the night air.
Silently he stepped through the brush, along the
bank of a small stream that met the big river further
down. Silver Wolf was right behind the leader, and
the leader's son was behind him. Then came Silver
Wolf's brother and mother. The old female had
stayed at the den to look after the pups, as she did
whenever the mother went hunting.

The leader climbed part way up a steep hill, crept
to a rock where he could look down on the ground
beneath him, and lay down, hugging close to the cool

granite. Silver Wolf did the same, and the other wolves bunched up around them.

The moon was up, and the forest was filled with silver light, almost as bright as day. At first Silver Wolf could hear sounds down on the forest floor, but he couldn't see what was making them. There were sounds of brush breaking, and the whimper and squeak of some animal.

Then two bear cubs rolled into sight, wrestling with each other, rolling head over feet. Both of them were the color of blue smoke, and they were very round and fat. In a moment the mother bear lumbered into the little clearing where the cubs played. She was big and shiny black, with a broad white streak across her chest. She walked with a flat-footed, awkward gait, cuffing her cubs when they rolled under her feet. She was intent on eating, tearing at the sedge that grew there, pulling it up greedily by the roots, and almost at the same time rooting in the ground for possible squirrels or chipmunks.

Sometimes the cubs stopped playing long enough to chew on the bark of a young pine for a few minutes. One of them jumped away from his brother and scampered up a larger tree, his brother right after him. The two of them peered through the branches at their mother below them. The hair on their noses and around their eyes was almost white, and their small black eyes were very bright. The mother seemed to be paying no attention to them or to anything but food, but all at once she lifted her head suspiciously and sniffed, swinging her head slightly back and forth. She had caught the scent of the wolves.

She looked up at her cubs and coughed and grunted. When they didn't respond at once, she reared up on her hind legs and shook the tree with her front paws. The cubs came tumbling down, squealing as they fell head over heels the last few feet. She cuffed them to make them move along with her. Walking fast, they disappeared among the trees, the cubs still yipping their indignation at being forced to move.

After the bears had gone, the wolf pack turned back to the trail and went home. Later that night, when the moon had gone down, a large animal crashed through the brush not far from the den where the wolf pups were, and the strong smell of bear reached the wolves. They never saw the bear, but in the morning Silver Wolf's mother moved her pups to the second den, and both she and the old female stayed close to them for several days.

eight

The pups were old enough to come outside the den now, and they spent the long spring days romping and sometimes squabbling. They liked to jump on Silver Wolf when he was resting, and chew his ears and bite his nose. Silver Wolf pretended to be angry when they did this; he would growl and nip at them, and their voices would rise to yelps and furious squeals. As soon as the pretended fight was over, they would snuggle up to Silver Wolf and go to sleep, their back fur wet and matted where the others had chewed on it.

One warm evening the leader took the pack hunting in a territory where they hadn't been for some time. It circled around to within about a mile of the trapper's cabin and then went on up the side of a mountain to an alpine meadow that lay just below a cirque brimming with fresh snow water.

They found a herd of deer in the meadow and managed to kill one of the older does. They ate well and lay down nearby to sleep. The next day they ate again, until the meat was gone, and then toward evening they started home.

Silver Wolf's brother was at the end of the line, and Silver Wolf himself was just ahead of him. When they had been traveling for some time, he heard his brother move off the trail. Silver Wolf stopped and looked back. His brother was sniffing at a chunk of meat that lay on the ground. He was more curious than anything else, for he had eaten too well to be hungry.

Silver Wolf gave a sharp warning bark, and in the line ahead of him his mother stopped and looked back. She too barked, and trotted toward the young wolf. But he had already sniffed at the meat and now he stepped forward to pick it up. There was a loud clang of metal as the trap was sprung. The wolf yelped in pain, his front right foot caught in the savage bite of the trap. He pulled and pulled to get loose, fear and pain in his voice.

Silver Wolf circled the trap, keeping a safe distance but looking for some way to get his brother loose. His mother moved in very carefully and sniffed at her son's mangled foot. She backed away hastily when the offensive smell of the steel trap filled her nose. Silver Wolf's brother strained to get loose, but the pain of pulling his injured foot made him moan and whine.

The rest of the pack went home, but for a long time Silver Wolf and his mother stayed with the trapped wolf, every now and then pawing at the trap, trying to find some way to set him loose. Toward dawn the mother went back to her den to feed her small pups, but Silver Wolf stayed with his brother.

Every now and then the young wolf tugged at his trap, and both he and Silver Wolf chewed at it with their strong teeth, but they couldn't make any impression on the heavy steel. Weakened by the loss of blood and by pain, the wolf lay on his side finally, his body heaving with labored breathing.

The sun came up and then clouded over, and a gentle rain began to fall. A pair of ravens flew to the ground near the injured wolf. Silver Wolf rushed at them and drove them, squawking, away. From the trees and sometimes from a safe distance on the ground, bright eyes peered at the trapped wolf, but none of the watchers came close.

When the sun had reappeared again and the moisture on the ground had begun to steam, Silver Wolf heard someone coming. He drew back out of sight and waited.

The man came into view, whistling, carrying a gun and a cloth bag. He stopped when he saw the wolf.

"Well, hello!" he said. "Got you, did I?" He laughed.

Silver Wolf's brother struggled painfully to his feet and looked at the man. He flattened his ears and snarled softly.

"Are you the chap that's been robbin' me blind?" The man came a step nearer. "I got no use for wolves, you know that? A bunch of thievin', murderin' scoundrels, that's what you are. But I can sell that coat, all right, all right." He leaned his gun against a tree. "Tell you what I think I'll do. I'll take you home and put you in the cage. Maybe your friends will come to call, eh? Maybe I'll get the whole murderin' lot." He laughed again and moved toward the wolf.

In the brush Silver Wolf lay flat on his stomach, tense and watchful. The hair on his back bristled, and deep in his throat he growled softly.

The man came toward the wolf very cautiously, holding the cloth bag spread out in his hands. He came on until the young wolf had backed up as far as the chain on the trap would let him go. Then the man sprang forward and covered the wolf's head with the bag. The wolf tried to struggle, but he was immobilized by the bag. Swiftly the man tied the bag tightly around the wolf's head, and then tied his hind feet together. He released the injured foot from the trap and tied it to the other front foot.

"There we go," he said. "That ought to do it." He slung the wolf around, and half-carrying, half-dragging him, he set out for the cabin.

Silver Wolf followed them, always out of sight of the man, but always with them. He watched as the man turned the wolf into the cage, untied his legs, took the bag off his head, and slammed shut the heavy wire door. For a minute the wolf lay still. Then he pulled himself to his feet, put his nose to the wire, and snarled. The man laughed.

"Don't like that, do you? Well, like it or lump it, you're staying there a bit till we see if the others come around. Then a nice, well-placed bullet that won't damage that pretty coat of yours. And first thing you know, some lady down in the city will be wearin' you around her neck. What a way to go!" Chuckling, he went into his cabin.

All day Silver Wolf stayed hidden in the woods, keeping watch on his brother. The man left the cabin and after a while came back again, carrying three trout. He built a fire inside the cabin, and Silver Wolf could smell the fish cooking. Then the man came out again and checked the hides that were drying on his rack. He took some of them down and went inside.

When it was dark, Silver Wolf left. He went home, and a little later he led his mother back to the cabin. His brother got to his feet weakly, wagging his tail. But the man, who was sitting in the darkness on his doorstep, remained motionless. From his place among the trees Silver Wolf could see the dull glint of the gun barrel. He and his mother stayed where they were.

It was hours later when the man rose, stretched, leaned his gun against the cabin, and went inside. Much later still, Silver Wolf's mother slowly crept out of the woods up to the cage. The two wolves touched noses, and the young wolf whimpered softly. The mother pawed at the wire cage and bit at it with her long teeth. At a sound from the cabin she instantly fled back out of sight. The man came out, rubbing his eyes and yawning.

"You had company?" he said to the wolf. "Any of your chums come around?" He stared into the dark woods. "Well, I ain't goin' into those woods to hunt 'em out, you can bet on that. They'll be back." He went into the cabin.

Just before dawn the two wolves went home. Silver Wolf's mother fed her pups and let them romp around her, but she was restless.

That night the pack hunted again, but Silver Wolf and his mother didn't go with them. Instead they went back to the cabin. Silver Wolf's brother was still in the cage. He still held his injured paw in the air, but he seemed stronger. Again the mother came to the cage and touched his nose, and again retreated when she heard the man.

On the third night they watched as the man came out of the cabin, fed a piece of venison to the wolf, and then tossed another chunk into the woods. He went back into the cabin and in a little while he came out with a flashlight and his gun and went off into the woods.

Silver Wolf's brother whined softly. After a long wait, Silver Wolf and his mother trotted down the path to the cage. The injured wolf wagged his tail and pushed his nose through the wire mesh. He tried to paw at the ground in the corner of the cage but he couldn't put his weight on his injured foot. Each time he tried, he lost his balance. Silver Wolf's mother began to dig on the outside at the same corner. She dug furiously, tossing up little clouds of dirt.

Silver Wolf joined her. The cage, a homemade one, had no floor. Instead, the wire sides had been thrust down about a foot into the ground to keep it from being pushed over by whatever animal was inside.

Every few minutes Silver Wolf's mother stopped digging and tugged at the wire with her teeth. Silver Wolf worked fast, all along the side of the cage,

shoveling the dirt with his paws, tearing at the wire with his teeth, listening all the time for the return of the trapper.

With a suddenness that almost threw Silver Wolf off his feet, the whole side of the cage lifted free of the ground. In a second Silver Wolf's brother was out. Running on three legs, he followed Silver Wolf and his mother through the forest toward home.

nine

The pups were beginning to be interested in chunks of meat now, and they liked to gnaw at bones. Silver Wolf helped his mother bring back meat for them, and they brought it too for his brother, whose injured leg made it hard for him to join the pack in hunting. He spent most of his time lying in the sun or in the warm rain near his mother's den, watching the pups play and waiting for his leg to heal. The little wolves enjoyed galloping around him, tumbling over him, chewing on his fur. Sometimes when they got too rough, he nipped at their floppy ears, but most of the time he let them play.

Silver Wolf left them one morning to look for food. He followed the river awhile and then took the path of a tributary that led to a lake. The sky was filled with billowing clouds, and a light southern wind rippled the surface of the lake. Although he couldn't see them, he heard the honking of geese overhead. On the other side of the lake, a moose splashed out into the water, looking for aquatic plants.

Silver Wolf sat there for some time. Far away, high in the mountains, he heard the faint boom of an avalanche and the rumble of snow crunching down the cliffs.

He watched a water ouzel walking along the bottom of the stream bed, looking for insects. The fat little bird walked upright, as if he were on dry land, stopping now and then to poke his beak into the wet sand at the bottom of the stream. He came up out of the water and perched on the long dead branch of a pine that hung over the creek. He looked at Silver Wolf, cocking his head on one side, singing his clear little song. Silver Wolf watched him till he flew away.

A magpie flashed past Silver Wolf, startling in his black and white plumage. Silver Wolf followed him, to see if he had found food. Two other magpies joined the first. Silver Wolf trotted faster, trying to keep them in sight.

He found them near a salt lick, picking at the remains of two whitetail bucks who had fought and locked antlers and eventually died, probably of starvation, unable to break loose from each other. They had been big bucks, with widespread antlers on which the last of the velvet still hung. The long cold of the winter had partially preserved them, but now in the warm weather there was little left except antlers, bones, and hide.

Hunks of wood torn from a nearby log during the fight lay beside them, and one of the tines of the larger buck had broken off in the body of the other.

The three magpies were hopping around the remains of the deer, looking for some bits of meat. When Silver Wolf came up, they lifted up a short way into the air, hovering, making their harsh sound, like a crow but higher, and chattering and whistling at Silver Wolf. He paid no attention to them, and in a minute they landed on the muddy ground again, long green tails twitching as they hopped about.

Silver Wolf sniffed all around the deer, but there was nothing left for him. He pulled loose a leg bone to take home to the pups to chew on. He was already away from the deer, pulling the bone through a dense thicket, when he heard the magpies squawk and flap into the air. He looked back to see what had alarmed them. Two men broke through the brush on the other side of the deer and stopped. They looked down at the deer.

"Not much left," one of them said, "except the antlers."

The second one walked around them. "Must have

been a good fight. And neither one of 'em got the doe." He laughed.

"I brought the Swede saw," the first one said. "We might as well take the racks." He pulled a long thin blade from his pack and knelt beside the deer.

Silver Wolf lay very still, watching, listening to the whining sound of the saw.

"Something's been here, recent," one of the men said. He pointed to the prints made by Silver Wolf's paws.

"Coyotes?"

The man bent down. "Well, they been here too, but that's not what this is. Looks to me like wolf."

The man who was sawing the antlers stopped to look at the prints. "You're sure as heck right. I'd like to get me a wolf. Make a nice rug when I get home."

"They're hard to get. I've never even seen a wolf, though you can hear 'em howling."

"I know a way."

"What?"

"That stuff I got for coyotes—1080."

"Will that kill a wolf?"

"Man, that'll kill anything. It'll even kill the birds and the animals that feed off the dead coyote, or dead whatever. That stuff really works." He looked around. "This'd be a good place to try it. Not only are the bucks here, but there's that salt lick. We'll give 'er a try." He went back to his sawing.

When Silver Wolf got home with the bone, the pups played with it, chewed on it, and fought over it for a long time. Even the leader joined in the game. The leader's son, who had been gone for almost a month, came home that evening, looking gaunt, a scar from a recent wound on his shoulder. He lay down, after the other wolves had greeted him, and wearily watched the play of the young wolves.

When the pack hunted, a few nights later, Silver Wolf found himself pushed out of the position behind the leader. Now that the leader's son was back, it was his place, and he made sure he got it. Silver Wolf dropped back to third place, but it was not where he wanted to be. If he had been leader, he would have taken the pack to a new site, away from the men he felt to be all around him. If anything happened to the leader, he would fight the leader's son for the head position, and he would take the pack far away.

ten

It was almost a week after Silver Wolf had found the dead bucks that he went to the place again, this time with his mother. They had been on a long journey in search of food, zigzagging around their territory for almost ten miles, before they started home.

On the way back, near the place where Silver Wolf had first seen the magpie, they found a beaver colony, and this time Silver Wolf succeeded in killing a beaver. He carried it in his mouth, taking it home for the young wolves and his brother. He was just ahead of his mother, and remembering the deer, he detoured to that spot, intending to get another bone. His mother would have to carry it because a fat beaver was all he could manage, but he

71

would show her where it was.

She trotted past him, stopping briefly to inspect the bones. The antlers were gone. She pulled a bone loose and carried it in her mouth, but as they started to leave, she turned aside, dropped the bone, and picked up a chunk of fresh meat. She ate part of it and carried the rest in her mouth.

They were near home when Silver Wolf heard a strange sound behind him. He turned and saw his mother. She had dropped the meat somewhere behind her; it was nowhere to be seen. She was retching violently. Silver Wolf went back and touched her with his nose. She shrank back and began to twitch all over. Her eyes rolled in her head, and in a few moments she went into convulsions. Silver Wolf stood close to her, whimpering and moaning. Foam flecked her muzzle, and he could no longer see her eyes. She shook with terrible shudders. She fell down and struggled to her feet again and again. Then her legs buckled under her and she couldn't get up at all. In a short time she was dead.

Silver Wolf lay beside her all night. Finally he went home, remembering to take the beaver. He gave it to the young wolves and his brother, but then, restlessly, he went back again to the body of his mother. The leader followed him, and the two lay close to her, whimpering quietly. Three ravens lay dead beside the body of the wolf.

When daylight came, the leader went back to the pack, but Silver Wolf stayed nearby, sometimes lying in the cover of tall ferns near the place where his mother was, sometimes wandering restlessly around the area. It was almost noon before he went home.

He returned to the spot that night, to find that his mother's body was gone, and there was a strong smell of man still lingering. He followed the scent for some distance before he lost it. For several hours he roamed, trying to pick up the trail again, but it was gone.

When daylight came, he went home. He was even more uneasy here now. The wolves in the pack huddled close to each other, and the pups whimpered. The old female had already taken over the care of the young wolves, and now the rest of the pack treated her with great respect. Silver Wolf lay down close to his brother, and the leader paced up and down. Back in the hills coyotes barked, and a soft rain pattered on the trees. The pups scuttled inside the den to get out of the rain. The old female lay across the entrance, her nose on her paws, ears alert to catch any sound of danger to her new family.

It was several days before the pack left home to hunt again. And except when he was on a hunt, Silver Wolf stayed close to the den for a long time, not going out by himself to explore and hunt as he had done in the past.

When the pups were about ten weeks old, the leader took the pack to a new home, north of the den about eight miles. They made the move at night, starting out right after sunset and continuing through the night until they reached the site. Part of the way the pups ran along, stumbling over every obstacle with their big floppy feet, stopping to play, running off to investigate new sights and sounds. The older wolves kept patient watch, waiting for them, bringing them back to the trail. Part of the time the whole pack rested while the pups, panting hard, lay down to catch their breath. Their feet and heads were big, compared to the rest of their bodies, and they easily lost their balance. When one pup seemed exhausted, the old female tried to carry him in her mouth, but he was too large for her. Now and then Silver Wolf picked up the smallest pup, one of the females, and carried her a little way, until she struggled to get down. It was a long night.

When they reached their destination, they found that the leader and his son had killed an old moose. That was why the leader had moved them to this new home. Other creatures had already been at the meat, and when the wolves arrived, a coyote went slinking off through the trees, his mouth full of food, but there was still plenty left. Hungrily, all the wolves ate until they could eat no more. The pups were too worn out to go for their share, and their teeth were still not strong enough to tear meat loose; but the older wolves saw to it that they had plenty to eat. The old female fed them before she ate anything herself.

After he had slept for hours, Silver Wolf set out to examine their new territory. It was the first time since the death of his mother that he had gone out alone. But he wasn't alone long. Within a few minutes his brother came limping after him. The brother's wound had long since healed, but the trap had taken off two of his toes, so he ran a little off balance and he often fell. Patiently Silver Wolf waited for him.

They explored country where they had not been before. After some time, they came to a high ridge, from which they looked down on a narrow dirt road that ran along a big lake. On the far side of the lake, the rocky cliffs rose even higher. But from the vantage point where they were, Silver Wolf and his brother could see enough of what was going on.

The woods were full of the cries of birds and the chatter of squirrels, who went about their business paying no attention to the motionless wolves.

Silver Wolf was staring steadily at the highest cliffs on the far side of the lake. He had seen some movement on a ledge. At first it was impossible to tell what it could be, but gradually he was able to make out the outlines of four bighorn sheep, their dark brown coats making them almost invisible against the rock of the ledge. Even from that distance he could see the white patch of their hindquarters and the white streaks that ran down their legs. They were eating, moving very little. Three of them were males, with large horns that curled around their heads; the fourth was a ewe, with slender, shorter horns. They were feeding on the sparse grass that grew in the crevices of the rock.

Silver Wolf watched them only from curiosity. Once he had tried to catch up with a bighorn sheep and he had found it was too difficult for him. The sheep had shot up the side of a steep rock wall as if it were running on level ground.

He watched them for a long time as they worked their way around the base of the ledge, eating steadily. Suddenly the biggest one lifted his head. At almost the same moment Silver Wolf, too, saw the man on horseback, coming around the bend in the road. The man stopped the horse and without dismounting, aimed his rifle at the sheep, sighting through the scope. But even before the sound of the first shot rang out, the biggest of the sheep leaped off the ledge to another one, lower down. He turned and jumped up to a higher rock face, and then with another leap, disappeared. The ewe and the two rams followed him, gunshot ricocheting off the rocks around them. When the last ram jumped to the small ledge, it gave way under him, but he spun his body around in midair and landed safely on a lower outcropping. In a moment he had disappeared too.

The hunter sat there on his horse for some time, scanning the mountainside through his binoculars. Finally he picked up the bridle, and his horse plodded on slowly down the road, sending up little clouds of dust from his hoofs. When the man on the horse was gone, Silver Wolf and his brother went back to their new home.

eleven

Silver Wolf and his brother stayed together all the time now. When the pack hunted, sometimes if the ground was uneven, the lame wolf would have to slow down, stumbling and falling. When that happened, Silver Wolf waited for him. Together they brought back food for the pups and the old female, who seldom hunted anymore. On the rare occasions when she did hunt, she would stop often and howl, then stand listening for the high answering howls of the pups.

Sometimes when Silver Wolf and his brother set out by themselves, the pups would try to follow them. Then the two older wolves would have to chase them back home.

One late afternoon when the rays of the sun

slanted in from the west through the pines, the two wolves started out together. Several times they had to stop and chase some of the pups back. The old female came and helped them.

They had reached the far side of a small clearing, skirting it as they had done all clearings ever since the day the plane had killed their sister. Silver Wolf stopped and looked back. Just coming into the other side of the clearing, the smallest of the male pups came galloping toward them. He tripped over a branch and sprawled, got up and came on again.

Silver Wolf gave a short warning bark and started back along the edge of the clearing, to send the young pup back.

When the little wolf was almost in the middle of the open space, the sky above the clearing seemed to darken. Silver Wolf looked up. An enormous golden eagle was diving straight down, from far up in the sky. His flight feathers outspread, his wing-spread almost eight feet across, he seemed to fill the whole sky. Before anyone had time to move, he swooped down on the little wolf, clasped him in his huge talons, swerved up again, and was gone.

Silver Wolf stood still, staring up into the empty sky. Hearing a low, mournful howl, he looked across the clearing and saw the old female. For several minutes she pointed her nose toward the heavens and howled. Then, lowering her head, she trotted back

to the other pups.

For a long time Silver Wolf and his brother lay beside the clearing, but after darkness came, they went back to the other wolves. The pups were restless and whining. The old female hovered over them anxiously. Whenever a pup started to wander off, she darted nervously after him and maneuvered him back to the others. It was a long time before she let any of them out of her sight again.

For several days, when the leader went hunting, Silver Wolf and his brother stayed behind, staying close to the puppies. But because the elk herd had moved back into the high country and the deer ranged freely on the land that was now free of snow, hunting was not easy for the pack. About a week after the eagle had carried off the pup, the leader moved the pack again, north and east, to the other side of the lake where Silver Wolf had seen the bighorn sheep. They settled into a grassy bank not far from the lakeshore, and the water lapping against the shore became a part of the sights and sounds and smells that they grew used to. Silver Wolf felt restless there. He carried in his head a feeling of danger, the memory of the man with the gun, who had shot at the sheep.

There were many things to explore in their new home. Silver Wolf and his brother went out almost every day, as well as at night when the pack hunted.

One of their favorite places was a burned-over area, where the tall skeletons of trees, fire-blackened, stood here and there, some of them still erect, some leaning against others. The ground was a tangled mass of dead brush and blackened earth.

At one end of this burned place, Silver Wolf found a red fox's den, in an abandoned woodchuck hole. The fine black dirt that led to the entrance was marked with the narrow prints of adult foxes and the tiny ones of the kits. Once Silver Wolf thought he saw a flash of rusty-red disappearing into the burrow, but although he could smell fox, he couldn't see into the dark hole, and no fox came out during the time he waited.

Sometimes there was food near the tunnel that he and his brother ate: a weasel, a mole, several birds, some of them partly buried, some just lying on the ground. And one day not far from the fox den they came upon a bear that showed signs of having been killed by a rival. His chest and shoulders had been badly raked. A silver fox was feasting on the meat, and the magpies and a big gray jay were there.

When they saw the wolves, the magpies flapped up into the air, and the jay sailed up to a limb of a tree, tipping his black-capped head and whistling at them in his loud voice. The fox trotted off to one side and waited to see what the wolves would do.

When they settled down to eat, he grabbed a piece of meat and ran off with it. The jay hopped up the branches of the tree, going around and around the tree, and then hopped down to the ground. After he had done this on two more trees, scolding all the time, he came back to the bear and ate.

Later Silver Wolf and his brother led the pack to the remains of the bear. This time even the old female came, soon hurrying home with meat for the pups. The male wolves too took home all the meat they could carry.

The weather had turned hot and humid but that night a smashing thunderstorm cleared the air. Silver Wolf lay in his bed, his nose between his paws, letting the cool rain soak into his coat. He lifted his head quickly when a thunderbolt smashed into the forest not far away.

Soon after the lightning had struck, the storm cleared. Silver Wolf sat up uneasily. He smelled the smoke of burning trees. The other wolves, too, tensed and sniffed the air, whining and looking at each other. Then they began to feel the heat and hear the crackle of flames. The forest was on fire.

twelve

The forest came alive in a rush of escape. First the birds came, filling the air with the beating of wings and their cries of anxiety. Then the deer, running recklessly, terrified. The smaller animals joined the panic-stricken flight—the squirrels and chipmunks, the rabbits, the mice, tiny gophers, three coyotes—both hunter and prey frightened by the common danger. A snowy owl flew past, and a bobcat dashed through the trees.

The wolves began running too, helping and pushing along the bewildered pups. The leader and Silver Wolf and his brother and the leader's son all helped the old female keep the young wolves moving. Through scratchy patches of juniper, through stands of spruce, across the old burned ground, along the

shore of the lake, they ran. Stumbling through buck-thorn, Silver Wolf almost stepped on a big hoary marmot, silvery gray and almost invisible among gray rocks, hurrying along and whistling his danger call. An elk thundered by, followed by three of his cows. A jackrabbit, his bright yellow eyes wild with fright, leaped out of their way.

In the lake many animals were swimming toward the far shore. Three moose were out in the middle of the water, their heads lifted high. Beavers were swimming away from their home, and the wedge-shaped heads of muskrats rose above the water. Frightened woodland jumping mice shot out into the water and swam frantically.

Black smoke billowed around the wolves, and the crackle and roar of the fire was close behind them. The heat was intense. The pups were panicky, trying desperately to get away from the peril that bore down on them. The older wolves pushed the young ones toward the lake and into the water. Frightened of this new danger, they struggled to get out again, but Silver Wolf herded them deeper until they began to tread water. The old female stayed behind them, and the leader swam out in front, going along the line of the shore but staying far enough out to escape the fire. Sparks and black soot fell all around them. Then with a great roar the fire reached the woods that bordered the lake where they swam. Dense, choking clouds of smoke billowed out over the water, and trees exploded into flaming torches. Burning branches fell into the lake with a hiss, some of them flung far out by the force of the exploding trees. A big blazing limb of a pine, with a terrified young squirrel still clinging to it, narrowly missed Silver Wolf's head and crashed into the water.

In the dense smoke and the dancing heat of the air, it was impossible to see more than a very short distance. Silver Wolf ducked his head under water when the searing heat and choking smoke became unbearable. He could no longer tell where the other wolves were.

When he surfaced again, the fire had gone on by, but the heat and smoke were still almost overpowering. He swam along parallel to the shoreline. The lake curved, and eventually he came to a place where the fire had veered away from the shore. He floundered onto a small sandy beach and flopped on his side, breathing hard. Even here, where the fire had not actually come, the ground was warm.

Once he was able to breathe normally, he sat up and looked around. A little way below him the leader and his son had come ashore, and heading toward them the old female swam, herding along the exhausted pups. They were all there, but the old female was pulling one of the females by the ruff on her neck, and the little wolf's eyes were closed. She carried her up onto the sand and laid her down. The leader came over and sniffed the little wolf all over.

Silver Wolf joined them. The little wolf opened her eyes, and after a moment she tried to get up, but something was wrong with her hind legs. Whimpering, she fell back again. The old female licked her all over but it did no good. The other pups, recovering quickly from their fatigue and fright, played on the beach, but she only watched them, her eyes half-closed. From time to time she tried to reach around and lick her hind legs, but the pain made her whine and lie back again. Silver Wolf sat beside her for a while, watching her.

Drowned and smoke-killed birds and small animals washed up on the shore. The surface of the lake was dark with streaks of soot. But after a time, a wind came up and ruffled the smooth surface, breaking up the concentrations of soot and bringing a cool relief to the animals on shore. Debris, broken and charred branches, twigs, leaves, washed up on the shore.

The air was still so smoky that it was hard to tell whether the sun was shining. Late in the afternoon a canoe came up the lake with two men in it. They came so silently and swiftly that there was hardly time for the wolves to climb up the bank and into the woods, out of sight. The old female tried to carry the injured pup, but the little wolf yelped in pain, and the old female, frightened, left her and scuttled up the bank into hiding.

The men in the canoe heard the yelp of the wolf and turned their canoe in toward the beach, their paddles dipping rhythmically and silently in the rippled water. They beached the canoe and got out. They were dressed alike, in tan shirts with an insignia patch on the arm, and tan pants tucked into heavy boots. They bent down to look at the little wolf. She looked back at them, in too much pain to be fearful.

"Looks like a drowned rat," one of the men said.

"A wolf pup." Cautiously the second man reached his hand toward her head. She pulled her lip back over her teeth but she made no attempt to bite him. "Take it easy, little sister, take it easy." He stroked her head.

"What's the matter with her?"

The second man crouched beside the pup and lifted her gently to her feet. She whimpered and pulled her hind legs under her. When the man touched her legs, she yelped in pain. "Looks like she broke her leg. Maybe both of them. All right, little wolf, don't panic. Nobody's going to hurt you."

"She'll never make it." The first man pulled a gun from the holster at his waist. "Better put her out of her misery."

"Hold it." The second man ran his hand over

the legs. "If I take her home, I can splint those legs. She might come through it o.k."

"Listen," the first man said, "this place is full of injured and dying animals, after that damned fire. You can't take 'em all home."

"No, but I could take this one."

"What'll your wife say?"

The man laughed. "She'll probably say, 'What do little wolves like to eat?' And she'll be so busy looking after it, she'll forget to ask how *I* am. Last year we brought up a fawn, and the year before it was a couple of fox kits." He went to the canoe, got a jacket, and made it into a sling. "Now, little lady, if you'll just lie nice and quiet in the bottom of the canoe, we'll be home before dark, and you'll get treated like a princess." To the other man, he said, "Wolves make good pets, if you get them young. They're a lot like dogs, after all."

"Well, I'm glad it's your pet, not mine." But the first man helped him get the little wolf into the canoe, where she lay quietly on the bottom. "She sure don't make any fuss."

"She may be in some shock. We'll have to watch out for that." He took off his shirt and folded it over her like a blanket. "O.k., let's shove off."

thirteen

The wolves had to find a new home. Most of their territory, including the trapper's cabin, had burned. All that night they traveled, following the leader, who always seemed to know where he was going. Toward morning they came to another lake, a very small one, far away from the area where the forest fire had devastated the land. A gently sloping hillside overlooked the lake, and at the top of this, sheltered by a thick stand of birch, the wolves once more set up a home.

The first night that the pack went out to hunt from their new base, Silver Wolf was uneasy. The old female had stayed behind with the young wolves, and every half mile or so, Silver Wolf stopped to howl and to wait for the old female's answering howl.

Each time he stopped, his brother stopped too, so that soon the leader and the leader's son were some distance ahead of them.

When they caught up with them, the leader and his son had stopped on a grassy slope that led down to a sheer drop of several hundred feet. Far below, a river thundered along toward the waterfall that they could hear but not see. Silver Wolf looked over the edge of the cliff, then drew back cautiously. He went to a clump of trees at the edge of the grass and sat down, his tongue lolling out of his mouth. The night was hot and humid, the sky overcast.

Near him the bright eyes of a curious raccoon peered from its tree hollow. Silver Wolf waited to see what the leader would do.

After a long interval the leader stood up, wagged his tail, and went to the other side of the grassy place, his son right behind him. In a moment Silver Wolf and his brother joined them. Below where they stood was another small clearing, where three antelope were feeding.

North of where the antelope were, a steep path covered with loose shale led down to the river. The little antelope ate nervously, looking around often, but they had not seen or smelled the wolves.

The leader moved nearer the edge, inching forward on his stomach. Silver Wolf turned his head sharply; he had caught the smell of bear. He looked again at the leader, and at the antelope below them. The grassy ledge where the antelope were was small. It would be possible to get trapped there, with no way out except down the steep path to the fast-flowing river.

Silver Wolf moved in front of the leader and pushed at him with his nose. The leader turned his head away and tried to crawl past him but Silver Wolf persisted, trying to stop the leader from making the attack. The leader hesitated. His son shoved at Silver Wolf, to get him away from the leader. For a moment Silver Wolf tussled with him, both wolves snarling.

Then, abruptly pushing them aside, the leader sprang off the cliff into the midst of the antelope, his son right behind him. Silver Wolf and his brother did not follow.

The fleet antelope leaped for the edge, but the third one never reached it. As the first two fled with sure footing down the precipitous path to the river, the leader caught the third one by the leg and threw it to the ground.

When the antelope was dead, Silver Wolf joined the other two, to eat, and his brother came last, sliding awkwardly down the cliffside with his three good feet. The leader's son snapped at Silver Wolf.

Each wolf carried part of the meat home for the old female and the young ones. Part-way home, Silver Wolf, who was the last in line, stopped and put down his meat and listened. Again he had the feeling of bear in the vicinity. He picked up the meat and went on, but he kept a careful watch.

The young wolves snapped at the meat hungrily, and the old female waited until they were through before she ate. Each wolf had made a claim to his particular piece of meat, and even though the smallest male had stopped eating, he went through a ritual of growling and pretending to guard his piece when the female touched it. She was patient with him, and in a few minutes he fell asleep.

Finally all the wolves slept. It was early in the morning, the cloudy sky turning faint gray, when Silver Wolf was awakened by a noise. He came to his feet at once, his hair bristling. The smell of bear was very strong.

He heard the grizzly before he saw him. The bear was thrashing around clumsily in the brush near where the meat had been.

All the wolves heard him now. The old female cuffed the young ones to keep them from getting into trouble. The four male wolves trotted toward the intruder. He was rooting in the ground, looking for the meat that he could smell. He was standing with his nose to the ground, his hump rounded between his shoulders. He was dark brown except for the grizzled ends of the hair on his back and shoulders.

Finally he heard them, and he jerked up his head with a surprised cough, turning his dish-faced head toward them as they charged him. He was about five times as big as any one of them, but he was clumsy and he was alone. He backed up in a series of awkward leaps as they closed in on him. The leader dashed in at the bear's flank, and as the bear turned to swipe at him with his huge front claws, Silver Wolf nipped at the bear's shoulder.

The grizzly kept backing up, and the wolves kept attacking. Sometimes the bear slapped with his claws —Silver Wolf's shoulder was raked by one such attack—but mostly the bear tried to grab a wolf between his big paws. Once he almost caught Silver Wolf's brother, but as he turned to ward off a painful bite from Silver Wolf, the brother escaped.

When the bear had been driven back several hundred yards, the wolves suddenly gave up the attack and returned home. The bear wheeled his huge bulk around and went off into the woods with his heavy rolling gait.

fourteen

The weather was unusually hot and humid for about a week. Twice the pack went out at night to hunt, but when they found nothing easily available, they came home again, lapping up the cold water at the lake and trying to find a cool place to rest.

Then the hot spell broke. A gentle rain cooled the air and relieved the oppressive humidity. The animals in the forest began to move around more freely.

Between showers at night, the leader took the pack out again. He led them back to the place where they had found the antelope. Again the scent of bear was strong in the area, but the wolves were too hungry to bother about the possibility of encountering the grizzly. If he came along, they could chase him off.

Moving ahead fast, the leader put some distance between himself and the other wolves. The old female had come along this time, and she was some distance behind the three young males—Silver Wolf, his brother, and the leader's son.

When they got to the cliff that overhung the river, the water, higher than ever from the recent rain, drowned out every other sound. At first Silver Wolf couldn't see where the leader had gone. He went to the edge of the cliff and looked down to the grassy slope where the antelope had been. There was no sign of any animals down there now. But he could smell fresh meat.

The leader's son trotted around the grass with his nose to the ground, then swerved off up the slope toward a grove of larch trees. Curious, Silver Wolf followed him.

At the edge of the trees the older wolf stopped. When Silver Wolf caught up with him, he saw the leader, hidden in a clump of trees, sitting very still. Beyond him, back to him, the grizzly was eating the remains of a goat. So intent was the bear on his food that he was not aware of the wolves. Silver Wolf's brother and the old female sat down a distance behind Silver Wolf and the leader's son, and all the wolves waited to see what the leader would do.

For a time he did nothing. The bear ate steadily, stopped and rubbed his great shaggy back against the bark of a tree, and went back to eating.

With a spring so swift that his body seemed to blur in the air, the leader attacked the rear flank of the bear. Surprised and angry, the bear wheeled around, growling, dropping the meat that he had just picked up. The leader grabbed the meat and sprang back into the brush, dropping it for one of the other wolves to pick up. The old female leaped on it and left the grove, carrying it home.

The big bear came with surprising speed toward the leader, who jumped aside just in time to escape the crushing hug of the outstretched paws. Now the leader's son joined in the attack, worrying the bear from behind, while the leader attacked from the side. Silver Wolf joined in, grabbing the long dense hair of the bear's shoulder. But when his brother tried to attack too, and stumbled, Silver Wolf withdrew.

A wide swipe of the bear's paw knocked the leader's son into a tangle of ferns, and with that enemy momentarily out of the way, the grizzly took out after the leader. Silver Wolf renewed his attack, to protect the leader, but the bear flung him off with a great shake of his body.

He thundered after the leader, chasing him into the grassy clearing. Near the edge of the cliff, the leader turned to face his attacker.

Scrambling to his feet, Silver Wolf leaped at the bear again, but the bear didn't even turn as Silver Wolf's teeth caught at his thick fur. Silver Wolf let go, backed off, and prepared to go for the bear once more. But before he could do it, the bear rushed the leader, and with his heavy body he shoved him off the edge of the cliff. The roar of the river far below them was so loud that they heard no splash when the leader's body hit the water.

Snarling and popping his teeth, the bear faced Silver Wolf and his brother and the leader's son, who had just now come from the woods, limping, his leg scraped to the bone by the bear's claws. The wolves held back. Growling and coughing, the bear went back to the meal that had been interrupted.

The three wolves found the steep path to the river that the antelope had used. Sliding and slipping, Silver Wolf and the two-year-old made their way down to the river's edge, while Silver Wolf's brother waited at the top. Both wolves stood peering down into the fast, foaming water that broke around the boulders and dead trees in its path. Just beneath them a whirlpool churned and tossed up its spray, wetting their faces. To their left they could see the rapids that came just before the falls. There was no sign of the leader.

Silver Wolf watched a partly decayed log swirling

down the river. It hit a reddish rock in the middle of the stream and shot straight up in the air, then fell back into the river and sped on toward the falls, twisting and turning. In a moment it hit the rapids, spun in a fast circle, and shot toward the falls. Then it was gone.

Silver Wolf started the difficult climb up the cliff, digging his sharp toenails into any crevice the rocks offered. He slipped backward on loose shale and tried again.

When he scrambled over the edge onto the grass, he started for home at a fast trot, his brother just behind him.

fifteen

For a few days the wolves stayed at home, not going out to hunt. But one night when hunger began to make them restless, Silver Wolf roused the old female, his brother, and the leader's son, and started out to hunt.

Almost as soon as they were on their way, the leader's son pushed Silver Wolf aside and took the lead. For about a mile Silver Wolf let him lead. Then he jumped a small stream ahead of him and took the lead again. The maneuvering for position went on for some time, with Silver Wolf's brother and the old female keeping their distance.

The leader's son was at the head when they scented a moose. They caught up with her in the shallow water of a stream that fed into a nearby lake. She was a tough old cow, and when she saw them, she bellowed, pawing the ground with her hoof and shaking her head. They couldn't get near her.

When she turned and ran out of the creek in a shower of water, they dashed after her. She galloped hard along the shore of the lake. A doe and two fawns, who were drinking at the water's edge, fled in terror as the moose and the wolves thundered toward them.

The moose was old, her legs stiff, and from time to time she stumbled. Once she almost fell, and Silver Wolf nearly caught up with her, but she staggered on, increasing the distance between them again, with her long gallop.

The chase went on for a long time. Ordinarily Silver Wolf and the older wolf would have given up, but now they were competing for leadership as well as food. Silver Wolf's brother and the old female had long since fallen behind.

In the darkness they sometimes lost sight of the moose, but they could hear her pounding hoofs. The moon came out and made a broad silver path on the dark water.

The wound the bear had made on the leg of the leader's son had broken open again and was bleeding. Both he and Silver Wolf were panting for breath. At last the older wolf faltered and fell on his side, struggling for breath. Silver Wolf kept going.

He would not be able to run at this speed much longer. But the moose was tiring too. He was close to her now, and he saw her stagger and almost fall several times. Then he was alongside her. But he was alone, no match by himself for a moose. Yet he stayed with her, harassing her flanks. She kicked out at him and missed.

She veered toward the lake so abruptly that Silver Wolf's momentum took him on past her. He heard the splash as she wallowed into the water and started swimming for the opposite shore. They were at the narrow end of the lake, where there was no great distance from one shore to the other. Without hesitation Silver Wolf ran into the lake too and followed her.

She kept her lead until just before they reached the shore. Then for a moment she stopped swimming and half-rolled on her side. Silver Wolf was almost up to her when she struck out again. She floundered out of the water onto a narrow sandy beach, bellowed once, and fell dead.

Exhausted, Silver Wolf lay on the sand beside her for some time. Then he sat up and howled. Answering howls came from the other side of the lake. In a little while the leader's son came, staggering with weakness. He gave Silver Wolf a long stare, and then ducked his head. Then Silver Wolf's brother and the old female came around the head of the lake. They ate—the leader's son and the others—but not until Silver Wolf, their new leader, had had the first food.

Later they slept. The next afternoon the old female and the old leader's son went back to get the pups. They brought them to the lake, and after they had eaten, Silver Wolf found a new site for them, not far from the bank of a stream that ran into the lake. Silver Wolf built his bed on the highest ground, where he could keep watch over his pack and try to protect them from danger. If man came, they would have to move again, but for now they would rest, and try to maintain their new home.

Suggestions for Further Reading

Collins, Henry Hill, *Complete Field Guide to American Wildlife: East, Central, and North,* Harper and Row, New York, 1959.

Crisler, Lois, *Arctic Wild,* Harper and Row, New York, 1958.

Frenzel, Jr., L. D., and L. D. Mech, "Wolf-deer Relations in Northeastern Minnesota" in *The Naturalist,* Spring, 1962, pages 8–9.

Hellmuth, J., *A Wolf in the Family,* The New American Library, New York, 1964.

Mech, L. David, *Wolf: The Ecology and Behavior of an Endangered Species,* Natural History Press (distributed by Doubleday), 1970.

Mowat, Farley, *Never Cry Wolf,* Dell Publishing Company (paperback in two volumes), New York, 1963.

Rue, Leonard Lee, III, *Sportsman's Guide to Game Animals,* Harper and Row, New York, 1968.

Young, Stanley Paul, *The Wolves of North America,* American Wilderness Institute, Washington, D.C., 1944.

Young, Stanley Paul, *The Wolf in North American History,* Caxton Printers Ltd., Caldwell, Idaho, 1946.